GALAXY DIARIES

ROD J. SPURGEON

OWN THE ENTIRE STARCRUISER
GALAXY COLLECTION
BY
ROD J. SPURGEON

———

Who Blew Up My Ship?

The Wereghost Menace

A Very Goober Christmas

The Vampire Clones of Clegz

Galaxy Chronicles

Galaxy Diaries

Brakka's Zombie Armada

Galaxy Diaries

ROD J. SPURGEON

CONTENTS

"Sticking our noses into other people's business is something my crew and I do on a regular basis. I usually try like heck to avoid it, but somehow, I always get dragged into someone else's mess anyway."

— *Captain Mintax*

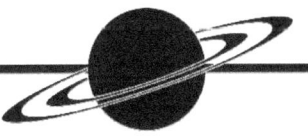

TRIP TO PROTEUS
FEATURING CAPTAIN MINTAX

Ship's log.

The only time I seem to make these things is when Goober does something like this, so unfortunately, I have a lot of them.

So, there we were on course to Proteus IV with a load of blasters when the Galaxy's warp drive went out—again. The Proteans intended to declare war on whatever group it was that insulted them this time, and they paid extra for fast delivery. They tend to threaten one star system or another so often without backing up their words with actions that the rest of the galaxy pretty much ignores their ranting. Don't tell them I said that though or they might stop buying weapons from me.

Anyway, we didn't have the part we needed

aboard ship to fix the drive, so I sent Goober in a shuttle to get a new one. I know what you're thinking, and no, I couldn't send Hitch or Steve instead. Hitch was working on repairing what she could on the drive without the part, and I needed Steve here just in case we were too tempting a stationary target for pirates to ignore. I could have gone myself, but there was no freaking way I was going to leave a million credits worth of handguns just sitting around in my cargo hold without me around to watch them. Yeah, go ahead. Call me a micromanager, but let's see how protective you get when you're stuck in the middle of nowhere in a galaxy full of pirates. I bet you'd stay close to your valuables too.

I considered sending Jonn, but he had to program a new startup sequence for the warp drive. It seems the core initialization program was damaged when the thing went out. That left Goober. It was either send him or use our sub-light engines to limp around space for the next year trying to get to the nearest spaceport.

So, off he went to get a new Apex wave modulation servo. It sounds like a simple task, doesn't it? Trek down to the local supply station, pick up a used part, and head back to the ship. The entire trip should have taken—

what—two days, at most? Well, he didn't get back for almost five. I still haven't figured out if he just flat out ignored my multiple attempts to contact him after missing the scheduled rendezvous. He claimed that communications must have been jammed and never got the call, but I have my doubts.

When he finally did get back, he was thoughtful enough to bring a few surprises along with him—three pirate ships. Apparently, he was overly forthcoming about why he was there and the cargo we were carrying with a couple of attractive girls that seemed very interested in what he had to say about egg cuisine. That should have been his first clue that something wasn't right with the situation.

Goober was wearing his favorite orange and yellow flower half-shorts and a green t-shirt with the words "Made in Uranus" emblazoned in bright yellow letters across his chest. Sounds like a great, eye-catching outfit that screams "date me." Right? Yeah, I didn't think so either. As it turned out, the girls were members of a small pirate faction that happened to be looking for their next conquest. Guess who they honored with that designation.

So, there we were, surrounded by three

Evvo class destroyers and we couldn't warp out of the area to avoid a fight. Did I mention that the weapons in the hold had a very volatile power supply? If those things shake too much during combat, or any other time really, they tend to explode. The pirates gave us the usual ultimatum—either give them our cargo or get blown up. You know, sometimes it really doesn't pay to get up in the morning. This was one of those mornings.

Fortunately for us, this particular pirate group wasn't the only one to glean a few unauthorized tidbits of information about our cargo from Goober. Just as we were telling those bastards what they could go do with themselves, another group of ships warped in and demanded the same cargo from us. It didn't take either group long to realize they were after the same thing. Since only one of them could have all the cargo, and there's no such thing as sharing the spoils of war among pirates, they started firing at each other. After a few minutes of watching them blow each other up, Hitch managed to get the part installed in the warp drive and we got the heck out of there as fast as our engines could manage. We found out later that neither group survived the fight. It just goes to show you that piracy doesn't pay, especially when you've got competition.

We ended up arriving only a week later than scheduled. That's a heck of a lot better than getting blown up and not arriving at all in my opinion, but the Proteans didn't quite see it that way. They wanted the weapons earlier in the week so their arrival would coincide with their annual cosmic cleansing celebration. Since they didn't have enough weapons to effectively threaten the latest offending group, they ended up making peace with them instead. Because that approach worked better than expected, they decided to take that same approach with their next annual celebration. It also means our regular contract to supply them with whatever weapons they choose to employ for their celebration was canceled. They liked trying new equipment each year and sold the old weapons back to us for a fraction of what they paid, so it was a massive blow to our yearly income. Fantastic.

Our biggest annual contract just disappeared overnight all because Goober couldn't keep his mouth closed. Ok, so there's a greater level of peace in the universe, and two pirate groups that used to rip people off were eliminated. Big deal. What am I going to do to replace that kind of income? I should have taken up terraforming. At least that pays a steady income, and since there are so many dead planets out there, it offers unlimited income potential.

Well, Goober's made an "I'm sorry" dinner to make up for losing the contract, so I guess I'd better get down to the lounge before it gets cold. You know, now that I think about it, maybe he didn't do such a bad thing after all, considering all the good that came of it. Don't you dare say a word to anyone about that though, or I'll deny ever having said it. I have a reputation, and income, to protect.

Mintax, out.

NO ACCESS
FEATURING CAPTAIN MINTAX

Ship's log.

It's been a little over a week now since it happened, and I'm still angry about the whole thing. Steve encouraged me to go to the shooting range to work off a little stress, and it's helped…a little. I can't get what happened out of my mind. Of all the stupid things to do. And to find out that it was Jonn, not Goober who did it. Goober I could understand. At least he has an excuse. He's Goober. But Jonn?

Locking down the ship and accidentally scrambling the biometric access system while almost everyone was on station sounds like sabotage. Not in this case though. I would have almost felt better if it had been the work of thieves or even a half-ass hacker. That way, I could go after them and kick their rears into the next millennium when I found them. Problem solved.

To tell you the truth though, I should have seen this coming. Jonn told me the Tagan program we—appropriated and integrated into the Galaxy's systems destabilized ancillary segments of code within the ship's computer core—whatever that means. He said it wasn't an issue and that he'd have it fixed after our trip to the station, so I guess it wasn't really my fault for believing him. Right?

Anyway, Steve, Hitch, and I left the ship after docking with the trade station. At first, I hesitated to leave Jonn and Goober on the ship without backup. We weren't exactly in the best of neighborhoods, and I'm not sure they'd be much better at defending the ship against attack than the crappy autopilot. I needed a strong showing during contract negotiations aboard the station though, and having Jonn and Goober with me instead of Steve and Hitch might not have been as impressive to a group of thugs that sell black market weapons to pirates for a living. Our potential clients were looking to transport borderline illegal torpedo components through a dangerous segment of space, and we needed to look as competent as possible. We're damn good at what we do, whether we look like it or not, so I don't care what you may have heard from *unreliable* sources.

After working past a few veiled death threats during price negotiations, we finally came to an agreement with the thugs. It was a chance for us to make 510,000 credits hauling one load of torpedo parts across 23 light years. It sounds more like a pleasure cruise than a job, I know, but that's not exactly how it turned out. In fact, it wasn't anything like that at all. Oh, it might have been, if we could get aboard our own ship. As it turned out, Jonn accidentally scrambled the security access system while trying to repair the core. We had absolutely no way to get back on board the Galaxy.

As you can probably imagine, that didn't sit too well with our customers. At first, they were somewhat patient while Jonn tried to fix the problem. Sure, the guy holding a blaster the size of his arm looked suspicious and eager to fire, but fortunately for us, he wasn't in charge. After stalling them for an hour though, their patience finally wore out. They accused us of lying about having a ship to fulfill the contract and that we were trying to cheat them out of the upfront payment. Hitch tried explaining to them that the only way we could have gotten on board the station in the first place was by ship, but they weren't buying it. That's when they drew their weapons on us.

Now, I consider myself to have average reflexes, but as soon as Hitch saw the...clients... reaching for their weapons, she pulled out her blaster pistol and had three of them on the ground before I could even lay a finger on my own gun. It brings a smile to my face knowing she has my back in a fight, but Steve didn't quite see it that way. He is our weapons specialist after all, and to be upstaged by the engineer—well, let's just say he wasn't too happy about it. He's still trying to challenge her to a "friendly" duel after that little display, with practice stun beams of course, but she refuses to give in to his bruised ego.

Well, once we fired our weapons and took out the bastards that tried to draw down on us, the station alarm sounded. The local authorities don't appreciate a firefight in their station—even if it is in self-defense. Well, not unless *they're* the ones doing the firing. Then, of course, it's okay. Typical.

So, there we were, about to be arrested

for breaking the "no firearms" policy aboard the station, and we had no way to get the heck out of there. Just as we started looking around for cover to try and hide, Goober called on the wristcom. I thought that maybe—just maybe—he had good news about the airlock. I can't remember the last time I received *any* good news, but as they say, there's a first time for everything. Well, this wasn't that time. Oh sure, Goober figured out a way for us to get back aboard the ship, but I would have almost rather taken my chances against station security.

You see, there is one port aboard the ship not directly linked to the security system. It's a little cramped and just barely large enough for someone to squeeze inside, but it's manageable. It also happens to be the old waste port before we switched to the current recycling system. I don't think the Galaxy's previous owners ever cleaned it out before I bought the ship, and I *know* I never cleaned out the thing afterward. Why bother, unless you happen to need to crawl through it for some ridiculous reason? Unfortunately, we had a pretty darn good reason. Incarceration really isn't my thing.

Goober managed to maneuver the ship and stick the port against the station's airlock.

I'm still amazed he got it right this time, especially since he ended up docking with a torpedo launcher at Syarko station a few months ago. Steve, Hitch and I crawled back aboard the ship, and we warped out of the solar system just as fast as we could before our disgruntled customers could come after us. I think I spent the next four hours afterward in the shower to remove the stench of that experience. One positive thing did come out of this mess though. The waste tube is about as clean as it's been since the ship launched for the first time more than 50 years ago. No, that's not even a minor consolation, but I'll take what I can get.

Well, reliving this experience has made my skin crawl again, so I'm going to hit the shower. Be sure to keep this event in mind the next time you think about neglecting your waste port. It might just prevent you from having to throw out your favorite jacket, should you ever need to crawl up the disgusting thing.

Mintax, out.

RACING LIBIDO
FEATURING CAPTAIN MINTAX

Ship's log.

You know, I love a good race. The competition. The speed. The thrill of victory. All except losing, of course. I really hate that part, especially losing a race because we're too busy running for our lives, thanks to the over-active libido of one of my crew. See if you can guess who that is.

The event started off well enough. Several dozen ships from around the galaxy signed up to compete in the annual Grali'k Nebulae Race. The race coordinators say it's supposed to promote peace by bringing the universe together in a friendly, spirited competition. Personally, I think the ruthless cutthroats in the race are just there to see how many ships they can "accidentally" take out. No matter who wins the race, though, the real winners are always the sponsors. Last year, they raked in more than 20 billion credits after everything was said and done, and they kept all of it for themselves. So much for bringing the universe together for altruistic reasons.

Personally, I don't really care why the race exists. I'm just in it for the cool million paid to the first-place winner. Yeah, I know. It's not much compared to what *they* haul in, but it's a heck of a lot more than what I've got in my pockets right now.

Anyway, we entered the Grali'k system near the nebula the night before the race. We cut our arrival a little close, but we had to finish a mission hauling electron sprockets to the Weladrians. It wasn't a very glamorous mission, but hey, whatever pays the bills. Right?

Despite my aversion to parties, we ended up having a good time at the pre-race meet and greet that night. It was a chance for fans to rub elbows with all the popular pilots in the race. It looked more to me like a frenzy of attention, which is something I *don't* want in my line of work. Anonymity has its advantages. If putting up with the social event meant earning a shot at a million credits with only a couple hours' worth of work, then I had no choice but to make an appearance. Just don't count on me to be cordial at these things or you've got another thing coming, and it won't be a smile.

Fortunately for me, the crowd seemed more interested in the pilots with the latest, shiniest ships. I happen to think the Galaxy is a very attractive ship, but in this case, I was willing to let their oversight slide—especially if it kept them from getting between me and the buffet table.

Toward the end of the night, I spotted Steve across the room with a rather attractive woman. What caught my attention was that she seemed to enjoy his company. I guess I expected a different outcome, since the last woman he tried to pick up actually picked him up instead—literally. She must not have liked his approach, because when he moved to place his hand on her arm, she grabbed it, twisted around and flipped him onto the ground. Hitch still reminds him of that now and then, and I can't help but smile just a little whenever she does.

It turns out that the woman Steve was…entertaining the night before the race was a pilot from another team. She must have been a pretty good one too because three fairly large corporations sponsored her. We came to find out that the companies were just shell entities run by a very powerful criminal cartel—one that wanted to know where their pilot was just before the start of the race.

Unfortunately, neither she nor Steve showed up that morning. They left the party together the night before, stayed out all night, and still hadn't shown up by race time. It wasn't a problem for us since Steve was just there as gunnery support in case one of the other pilots got too frisky. For the other team though, well, they weren't very happy about their missing pilot right before the race. You see, the cartel had a *lot* of money on the line for her to win. That's probably why they contacted us to find out what we did with her.

One of the cartel's goons saw her leaving the party with Steve, and since Steve is part of my crew, they naturally assumed I was responsible for her disappearance. Sometimes I wish people would just stop assuming the worst in others. Although, if the cartel did that, I guess they wouldn't be just another bunch of mindless thugs without a reasonable thought among them. Would they?

So, there we were at the starting line waiting for the race to begin. The Galaxy was running better than it had in months, thanks to Hitch and Jonn's upgrade efforts. Our timed trials were spectacular, and I think we had a good shot at flying away with a win *and* a million credits. Instead of dashing forward when the race began like we should have done, we ended up flying in the opposite direction.

No, it wasn't piloting error. I decided to fly the ship myself for this event, just in case. Two large cartel battlecruisers came straight at us with a solid weapons lock. I guess they didn't believe me when I told them I had no idea where their pilot and my weapons specialist were located. That's when they threatened to blow up my ship unless I handed their pilot over to them. Since there was no way I'd let that happen, I did the only thing I could. We turned the ship around and took off in the opposite direction. I don't usually run away from a fight, but sometimes a strategic withdrawal saves a lot of money in unnecessary repairs.

As we bolted away from the much larger ships, Steve *finally* called in. He said that he and his new "friend" had stayed out all night in a private shuttle orbiting a gorgeous planet that had fantastic cloud formations. I'm sure it was very scenic, though probably not as striking as seeing a barrage of 12 colorful energy beams trying to rip apart my ship. I immediately attempted to contact the cartel to let them know what happened, but they refused to take my call. If you're ever in a position where someone might have taken something from you, make sure you answer their call to see what they have to say. It might actually be *good* news.

Lucky for us, the Galaxy was faster than those lumbering behemoths. We ended up flying around the nebulae for nearly two hours before they finally gave up the chase. It wasn't long after that when Steve called again. He told us that he had dropped off his companion at her ship and was waiting for us at the finish line. If only he could have done that *before* the race started. Timing really is everything.

In the end, race officials disqualified us for obvious reasons, but the sponsors did give us an "I Survived the Grali'k Nebulae" award for making it out of there alive. The award came with a cheap duratanium trophy base with a crappy holographic image of a gas cloud above it. They also gave us a supply of 500 units of StimCap for participating. Goober was pleased, as it was his favorite energy drink. I wasn't. Still, the coordinators invited us back next year since we were at least mildly entertaining to the audience during our evasion of the battlecruisers. *If* we do return, I'm going to make damn sure to confine Steve to the ship until the race is over. Even that might not be enough to keep him out of trouble, but it's better than nothing.

Mintax, out.

HIT AND RUN
FEATURING CAPTAIN MINTAX

Ship's log.

Have you ever wondered why a criminal bothers to flee the scene of a crime anymore? Every government-protected sector of space seems to have DNA scanners these days. It's virtually impossible to get away with anything in secured space, and criminals almost always get caught, sooner or later, unless you're a pirate with a DNA scrambler, of course. They tend to get away with almost every underhanded scam they try to pull, except when they think about pulling it on me. They only tried that once, and I've never had a problem since.

So, you'd think that with as many ways there are to catch a crook, it would be impossible for the police to accidentally bust the wrong person for a crime. Right? Well, you'd be wrong.

Two days ago, when my crew and I left the Bolari system on a new job, everything seemed to be going well—almost too well. We were hired by a group of colonists to transport a load of geomite to Lotan V. The colony made the unfortunate mistake of settling on a planet with an atmosphere that kept bleeding off into space. Instead of relocating, they chose to reseed the planet's atmosphere every two years with geomite to stimulate its regeneration.

The colonists told me their previous hauler quit unexpectedly. They needed a replacement immediately, and my ship was the closest in this sector of space. It sounded like a nice, easy job—something we haven't had in a long time; but when they offered us 25 million credits to do it, I should have known something wasn't quite right, especially since the destination was less than a light year away.

You know what they say about a deal that looks too good to be true. Well, it's hard to look at it too closely when someone's waving 25 million credits in your face to do something that will take less than a day to do. So, of course, I took the job. "What could go wrong?" I asked myself, as I always do in situations like these. It only took an hour after leaving Bolari to find out.

Just when I thought my luck was finally changing for the better, Tioran Federation police showed up in three interceptors and ordered me to power down my engines. I hadn't broken any laws recently—as far as they should know, anyway, so I stayed on course and told them they had the wrong ship. Apparently, they thought they had the right ship and started firing on mine.

Since they wouldn't take my word that my crew and I were innocent, I had no choice but to shut down my engines in the middle of open space. Normally, that would be a bad thing with all the freelance pirates roaming this sector. With three police interceptors surrounding my ship, however, I doubted even the dumbest of scumbags would dare to attack. Of course, I have overestimated their intelligence before, so you never really know.

Anyway, when the police sent a small army aboard my ship to search for evidence of whatever it was they were looking for, their commander boarded my bridge and sat in my chair—*my chair!* Nobody sits there but me. Who the heck did he think he was, the Emperor? That's when he finally decided to tell me why he stopped my ship.

It seems the colonists reported that a crew from a vessel matching the description of mine boarded their freighter, stole all their geomite, and used the hull of their ship to ram the transport into the atmosphere. That's supposedly when their helpless cargo hauler burned up on reentry.

Have you ever heard such a load of crap in your life? As much as that story reeked of deceit, the police bought into it and searched my ship for the missing cargo. Guess what they found.

I told the police commander we had a valid contract for the geomite, but when I showed him the data crystal with the agreement, the damn thing was empty. That's when I found myself in a mobility restraint—*me!* Arrested and bound like a common criminal. Fortunately, there was nothing common about my programmer. When Jonn inspected the crystal, he found the colonists had planted a virus that deleted the data just after we left the Bolari system. How convenient.

Unfortunately for the colonists, Jonn makes redundant static copies of data in an isolated archive. The system detected the virus and eradicated it, allowing me to show the police our archived copy of the geomite contract.

I'm not sure what disappointed the commander more: getting duped by colonists in a scam to get free transport for their cargo or having to leave my chair. I'm guessing the latter. It really is a nice chair.

When those officers finally left my ship, Goober told me that if we had bashed into the transport, there would have been at least some damage to our hull—the most obvious hole in the colonist's story, and I didn't catch it. Couldn't he have told me that before the police arrested me? Well, at least he told me when we were alone on the bridge. I'd have never heard the end of missing that detail if Steve figured it out. He may be a good weapons specialist, but he can sure be a pain when he wants to be.

Remember this incident the next time you sign a contract. Make plenty of extra copies for yourself to make sure you don't get screwed by greedy scammers.

Mintax, out.

CAPTIVE SENTIENCE
FEATURING CAPTAIN MINTAX

Ship's log.

Sticking our noses into other people's business is something my crew and I do on a regular basis. I usually try like heck to avoid it, but somehow, I always get dragged into someone else's mess anyway. I occasionally wonder if I should even bother resisting since trouble is usually the inevitable outcome of waking up in the mornings…if it even bothers to wait *that* long.

While traveling to a business meeting for a potentially profitable mission a few days ago, Goober intercepted a weak distress call. Standard communications relays might have missed the transmission, but Jonn's adaptive algorithm allows detection of even the faintest signals. All I wanted to do was get to the business meeting on time and snag our best mission of the year. With a score that profitable staring us in the face, I should have realized that something else was bound to come along and screw it up.

We soon discovered that the signal was faint for a reason. A sentient android crew was forced to work for the Alisian Cartel aboard one of their gunship patrol vessels. The cartel is a nasty group of ruthless thugs, but they usually manage to exercise their dastardly intentions with surprising moderation. I guess they want to attract as little attention to themselves as possible, which is a smart thing to do since the recent cartel wars wiped out most of their competition.

The androids had been stuck serving the cartel against their will for more than five years. The crew on this particular ship turned out to be what was left of the Solar Flare, a former forceball team that had some of the better players in the Galactic Forceball League. I used to enjoy watching a good forceball game now and then, especially the championship Super Force game, but the sport just doesn't have the same aggressive appeal as it did nine years ago. That's when holographic players replaced the androids. I can appreciate that it's far less expensive to maintain holograms than androids, but watching a hologram getting ripped apart on the field just seems fake to me. I'll take a good android battle over that fake garbage any day.

Most forceball fans are aware of the well-publicized reason for discontinuing android players in the game. I have a few connections they don't, however, so I know the real reason behind the switch to holograms. To make the androids as successful as possible on the field, their owners designed their artificial intelligence to grow and adapt over time. That allowed the androids to make most of their decisions for themselves, and one of those decisions was that they wanted to get paid for their work. That turned out to be a bad move on their part.

Since the league wants to squeeze every ounce of profit out of as many fans as possible, paying for android players wasn't even a consideration. The organization just ended up booting them from the sport, forcing most of the androids to look for work in one dangerous, dead-end job after another.

My engineer, Hitch, felt sorry for the androids since she dated one a while ago. The star quarterback of the Asteroids was designed to be physically appealing to the audience and draw in greater ticket sales. All he ended up talking about during his time with Hitch, though, was his glory days in forceball. So much for that adaptive programming.

After a couple of weeks, Hitch broke up with him. She told me that was she was looking for more in a man than just physical attraction. If that were true, why did she spend two entire weeks with the guy? I guess I'll just never understand women.

Anyway, I knew Hitch wouldn't forgive me if I ignored the call for help, so I ordered Jonn to plot an intercept course for the gunship. The cartel probably wasn't going to just hand over its cheap laborers though, and I had no idea how we were going to free the androids. Steve offered a suggestion that only he could come up with to solve the problem. Hitch protested at first, but after I had pointed out that it was her idea to rescue the androids in the first place, I asked her to come up with a better idea. That's when she relented.

Jonn adjusted the Galaxy's heading to put us directly in the path of the gunship's projected course. When we arrived at the coordinates, we didn't have long to act. Jonn manipulated the ship's thrusters to put it in a gentle, but uncontrolled spin. Goober powered down non-essential systems and vented a small stream of plasma from the stardrive. Hitch left the bridge to get ready for her part in the plan.

Within ten minutes, the gunship arrived. Steve, Jonn, Goober and I moved into the conference room while Hitch pretended to run a diagnostic on an engineering console in the bridge. Steve and Jonn moved at a slower pace into the adjacent room while they casually gawked at Hitch in her new outfit. No, that's not accurate. Jonn casually glanced at Hitch. Steve unabashedly stared at her and whistled. Hitch made an appropriate gesture in response.

When the gunship hailed, the guys and I watched Hitch's interaction with them on a muted, split-screen connection. There were only three cartel thugs aboard the ship, and it didn't take much convincing to entice them over to help with repairs, especially since Hitch was wearing a revealing bikini top and skin-tight shorts that didn't leave much to the imagination.

After the cartel shuttle docked in our hangar, Goober sealed the inner and outer doors of the bay. Jonn activated a localized scattering field to block any communication transmissions from the thugs. The field also neutralized remote access to control chips embedded into each android. When we finished locking down the thugs in their shuttle, Hitch informed the androids they were free to go. I would like to have seen if the gunship had anything we could use, but it warped off before I could even bring it up. Selfish android bastards.

We ejected the shuttle soon afterward and warped off to our business meeting. Unfortunately, this little delay forced our contact to find an alternative service provider. Our biggest score of the year was just flushed down the refuse tube. Fantastic.

Before I recorded this log, I did receive some unexpected good news, for a change. The androids we freed are trying to build their own forceball league using money from the sale of the gunship. They sent a special "thank you" transmission for our help as well as a promise to supply us with a set of permanent use tickets to as many games as we want, once the league was up and running. I wish them all the luck in the universe, especially since I intend to collect.

Mintax, out.

EXPLOSIVE FANATICISM
FEATURING CAPTAIN MINTAX

Ship's log.

I've never considered myself a hero. I go in, do a job, and get out. No hassles, and definitely no fuss. Anonymity has its advantages in my line of work, but when it becomes necessary to break that anonymity to pull someone's butt out of a fire, it can also mean getting screwed out of a paycheck.

A few days ago, my crew and I were delivering a shipment of ammunition to a small group of self-proclaimed Great Protectors of the Cosmic Collective. I didn't care what the heck they called themselves, as long as they paid me for the shipment they ordered. The guns on my ship don't use the ammo they wanted, and there were no refunds from the black market shop where we bought them.

A few minutes before we arrived at the scheduled rendezvous, they changed the meeting location. It was only another two minutes further out, so I was willing to accommodate them. Getting stuck with a cargo hold full of useless ammo was less than an appealing prospect, so I didn't really have a choice in the matter. Bastards.

When we showed up at the new location in the middle of nowhere, six Collective frigates were circling a large mining ship in an asteroid field. One of the Collective ships broke off its orbit and approached us. The representative thanked us for the delivery and jettisoned a canister of credits, expecting us to do the same with the ammo. I had no intention of just handing over the cargo until I verified that every last credit they agreed to compensate us with was in that container. It never pays to be too trusting out here. I've known too many freelancers who found that out the hard way—if they escaped the encounter at all.

After Goober finished scanning the container and verified its contents, I was about to order the release of the ammo when Hitch redirected my attention to the

Collective swarm.

The single mining ship they were orbiting was larger than most. We scanned the ship and found out that it was designed for deep space drilling in hostile environments. It also had a small contingent of drone fighters for protection. That little fact didn't seem to matter though since the Collective blasted the drones apart with a little effort.

I contacted the Collective representative again and asked about the mining ship. The representative told us that desecrating the sacred mineral bounty given by Mother Cosmos was an attack on her celestial embodiment. They intended to destroy the defiler unless the captain agreed to pay tribute to Mother's benevolence. Chances are, they would have killed him either way, but it's usually more profitable to get the cash first before taking out a target.

I know some of our clients aren't exactly upstanding citizens, but these nutballs were about to kill a guy for trying to make an honest living. The miner's hull was down to 60 percent integrity and wouldn't last much longer under intense fire from six Collective ships.

The smartest thing for us to do at that point would have been to grab the loot, dump the cargo, and get the heck out of there. Do you think that's what we did? Of course not. Minding our own business is not something we're particularly good at, and this wasn't going to be an exception.

I told the guy to release the mining ship so we could finish our transaction in peace. I'll never forget the crazed look that appeared on his face after that. This was the first time I think I've ever seen someone actually transform from a reasonably sane individual into a raving lunatic in less time than it takes to sneeze. He started spouting cosmic revelation verses, using wild gestures to emphasize his words. When he finished his diatribe, he insisted that I deliver the cargo and leave the area. To help make his point, two of the ships orbiting the mining vessel broke off their engagement and started orbiting us.

Now, nobody tells me what to do, and I'm not easily intimidated, but our odds of victory in a six on one situation were less than favorable. We're good, but we're not indestructible, despite what you might have heard about us.

We needed an edge, something to help us even the odds. The mining vessel wasn't going to be much help, and any military support would have taken hours to arrive, if they even bothered to show up. We were on our own. A strategic withdrawal was still an option at that point since the Collective hadn't locked down our ship with a warp inhibitor. My crew wasn't exactly thrilled with that option though since it meant leaving the miner to die.

That's when Goober suggested something just as crazy as the Collective's method of persuasion. The asteroids in the area were composed of a mix of minerals, including the volatile Guratanium. As long as it remained in the cold depths of space, it was fairly stable. When exposed to extreme heat, however, anything near it wasn't likely to remain in one piece for long.

Sometimes the only way to fight crazy is with a similar measure of insanity. And if there's one thing we're good at, it's harnessing the improbable to improve our odds.

Hitch boosted power to the shields while Jonn casually moved the Galaxy as far away from a massive asteroid in the center of the field as possible. When Steve fired the lasers at the asteroid, nothing happened. We continued firing at the asteroid to agitate the Guratanium, but it had the effect of agitating the Collective as well. They may be overzealous fanatics, but they're not stupid.

The three Collective ships near us immediately opened fire, but they only managed to get off a few shots before the asteroid finally exploded. Our shields held, barely, and the mining ship's remaining armor withstood the explosion fairly well. The collective ships weren't so lucky. I guess they relied on the Cosmic Protector to defend their righteous indignation because their emaciated armor crumpled under the punishing force of the explosion.

All of their ships were disabled from the blast, giving the mining ship a chance to warp out of the area. That bastard didn't even bother to send us a thank you for the help *and* nearly getting our butts shot off while doing it. Can you believe that? That's gratitude in this self-centered universe.

Before we left the area ourselves, we moved to retrieve the container holding our payment. We weren't going to come all that way for nothing, and as far as I was concerned, we earned those credits. Unfortunately, the asteroid explosion blasted the damn thing apart. We were screwed again and stuck with useless ammo we'd have a hard time selling to anyone else.

It wasn't a total loss. In fact, we ended up making a small profit for our troubles.

Goober had the presence of mind to scan the asteroid rubble and recovered a small chunk of kelitronium. The extremely rare and durable mineral fetched a healthy price on the market, and after we had sold the ammo for scrap, we ended up with 165,000 credits more than when we started. I guess it's better than nothing—barely.

Sometimes doing the right thing isn't easy, but if you find yourself with a bright side to a bad situation, grab hold of it and hang on. It might be the last one you see for a while.

Mintax, out.

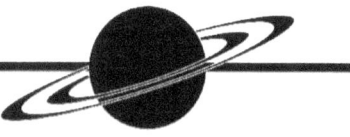

BACKSTABBING DOPPELGANGER
FEATURING CAPTAIN MINTAX

Ship's log.

I am extremely angry with myself right now. I can't believe I allowed myself to be taken in by that bastard when I should have seen it coming from light years away. Greed has a way of blinding people to the obvious; even when it becomes clear things aren't going to end well.

Last week, our injector system fused open in the forward port thruster while landing on Delta Zeta. That forced too much power into the thruster during a hard burn, and the damn thing blew up before landing. We fired up the Galaxy's main engines to return to orbit, but the damage was done.

The thruster was an original component

that came with the ship more than 50 years ago, so getting a replacement wasn't going to be easy. Steve mentioned that he'd heard of someone at a station not too far away that specialized in older technology. He swore that the guy could get us whatever we needed, which is usually the first sign that we should stay as far away from him as possible. As much as I wanted to tell Steve thanks, but no thanks, we needed that thruster to deliver a load of terror beetle excrement to the colony on Delta Zeta. Don't ask…just, don't ask.

The crew and I docked the ship inside the massive StarTropia station, one of the main hubs for exotic and hard to find items in this sector. When we approached the shop, I was a little put off by its name. Antique Collectibles doesn't exactly sound like a parts store for a working starship. The Galaxy might be old, but it's a fine starship that was a state-of-the-art marvel when it first launched, and I better not hear anyone say otherwise.

The store was surprisingly clean and modern. It had genuine hardwood flooring and shelves adorned with polished metal accents, creating an inviting atmosphere. There was even a sitting area with plush furniture one would normally find in a coffee shop. The place seemed more like a front for some business other than a used parts store. As long as the guy had what I needed, though, I didn't care what other business he was into. That turned out to be my second error. The first was listening to Steve about the store owners reputation.

The proprietor looked normal enough. He had an average height with a slender build and wiry goatee. His clean tan and white striped apron made him look like a barista rather than a purveyor of old equipment. I felt a nagging suspicion that something wasn't quite right about this situation, but when the man smiled and pulled out a cylindrical thruster slightly less than one meter in length from under the counter, my only thought was "how much?" That's exactly what I asked him, and to my surprise, he said 10,000 credits.

In the unlikely event you're not familiar with component pricing in this sector, that's cheap for a working thruster. The thing usually goes for 100,000 or more, depending on its rarity, and the one we needed was in that ridiculously rare category. I told him there had to be a catch, but he insisted there wasn't one. He needed the room in his shop for a new shipment of inventory due to arrive soon and told me I was doing him a favor by taking it off his hands.

I gestured for Goober to pay the man, but the merchant held up his right hand in protest. He told me he had been scammed recently when someone used fake currency to make a large purchase. That experience forced him to change his purchase policy to only accept electronic transfers for payment. The explanation made sense at the time, so I agreed. I only had a bit more than 11,000 in a Miners Guild and Trust bank account anyway, so even if it was some a scam and he took me for everything in the account, I'd still be getting a great deal on the thruster.

I placed my hand on the DNA scanner pad he held out toward me, and that was it. He shook my hand and told me to come back anytime.

When we got back to the ship, Hitch installed the thruster in 20 minutes without a problem. The unit worked perfectly, and output levels were in line with expectations. The process was surprisingly smooth, and we'd still end up making a profit on the Delta Zeta mission even with the unexpected expense of a used thruster. Do you want to know what else was unexpected? The security clamp latched onto our forward landing strut.

Clamps are only used by security forces to detain ships for acts of aggression, failing to pay docking fees, and, oh yes, theft. We quickly found out that it was this last reason that had us locked down with an armed team of security troops approaching the ship.

As it turned out, the merchant had altered his own DNA and appearance to mimic mine. He made a copy of my DNA when my hand pressed against the payment pad and used that data to alter his appearance to gain access to the Miners Bank. Only current and former Miners Guild members and their families could open accounts at the bank, or get past security into the building. The merchant used my access, and the threat of detonating a sophisticated bomb, to force the manager into transferring 10.2 million credits to another bank account.

Naturally, security had a few questions to ask me about the incident, and they felt the need to send 50 armed troops to ensure my compliance. If Goober hadn't convinced me to stop at a Frosty Freeze stand for an ice cream delight on the way back to the ship, the security scanner at the stand would have never picked up my presence there at the same time the robbery took place. The thief wanted to make sure I was still on the planet when he robbed the bank so the crime would be pinned on me. He never anticipated Goober's sweet tooth spoiling his getaway.

After four hours of interrogation, and finally catching the bastard trying to escape on a passenger shuttle, the police finally released me.

The next time Steve suggests using a friend of a friend that knows a guy to help with something we need, I'll know exactly where not to go. Sure, we may have retrieved the thruster we needed, but there's little sense in making a bad situation worse than it already is.

Let this experience be a lesson to you. *Never* allow greed or a preference for discounted merchandise to get in the way of caution, or you might find a fondness for ice cream as your only alibi against the criminal intent of a backstabbing doppelganger.

Mintax, out.

DOUBLE DATE
FEATURING ANDRE GU'BER

Ship's log.

Hello. Goober here. The captain asked me to record an entry in the ship's log since the, um, incident involved me. Well, he actually said it was my fault, but I don't have to add that part, do I?

Anyhow, it all started when we were on vacation on the planet Bentazi Urama. I know people sometimes call it the galactic cesspool of thieves and smugglers, but it really is a nice place to visit once you get used to it. Just be sure to leave anything valuable aboard your ship. Trust me on that one. I had to learn the hard way. I never did get my Uki droid back the last time we were here. Those are the cute, one-foot-tall droids that do all kinds of helpful chores, in case you didn't know. Jonn said I probably left it switched on and it walked back to the dealer, but I don't think so. Why would anybody sell something and take it back afterward? What's he going to do, sell it somebody else? Yeah, I thought it was a silly idea too.

When we went back to the planet this time, Steve had set up a date for himself the first night we arrived. I'm not sure how he does it, but since his dates can end badly, or worse, I'm not so sure I really want to know. This time, though, his date had a friend she wanted to bring along. Since Jonn was busy with some sort of cyber intrusion contest, Steve asked me to go with him. I was going to say no so I could visit the droid dealer and find out if he had seen my Uki, but Steve promised he'd buy all the drinks I wanted if I went with him. Do you know how much drinks cost down there? I couldn't say no to that offer. Right?

So, I put on my best lime-green shirt with awesome dark blue trim and headed to the club with Steve. When we got there, I couldn't believe my eyes. People were absolutely everywhere. They were so packed together, I bet they could tell what was in each other's pockets. If that was what the club owners wanted as a way to prevent people from bringing in weapons, it certainly didn't work, but I'll tell you more about that later.

Steve tried to tell me something, but the thumping music was so loud, I couldn't understand him. He finally gave up and gestured ahead. I guess he had been to a few of these places before because he moved forward through the crowd as though they weren't even there. I just followed behind him as close as I could so the crowd wouldn't swallow me up, and it worked—barely.

When we finally got to the bar, he introduced himself to two attractive girls. They were wearing tight dresses that showed off more than I thought people could show in public. Don't get me wrong, I'm not complaining, but do you know how hard it is to maintain eye contact when the person you're trying to talk to is wearing something like that? Believe me, it wasn't easy, and I might have even peeked a time or two, but it's not my fault. Is it?

I introduced myself to the ladies, but the music was so loud, I couldn't understand what they said back to me. I just smiled and nodded so they wouldn't think anything was wrong with my hearing. It's important to make a good first impression.

After introducing ourselves and getting a couple of drinks, the ladies gestured for us to follow them to a more secluded section of the club. I'm not so sure you could call any place there secluded, so let's just say it was a little less crowded than everywhere else. When we got there, they encouraged us to dance with them. I may not be the greatest dancer in the universe, but I have picked up a few moves here and there. Well, that's what my Dance Conqueror program told me the last time I used it anyway, so it has to be true.

When we started dancing, I thought the girls were very friendly and outgoing, since their hands were all over Steve and me. I didn't feel right doing the same, so I just pumped my arms in the air while moving from side to side. Steve didn't have the same reservations I did, but after a minute of dancing with his date, he got a curious look on his face. That's when things took a turn for the worse.

The two ladies turned to each other and nodded. They pulled out small pistols from under their dresses and pressed them into our stomachs. I guess the girls didn't expect Steve to find out about the hidden weapon so soon, but they didn't know how, uh, sociable he could be.

Steve's date ordered him to transfer the credits from our latest score to their bank account. I found out later that Steve wanted to impress the woman he had met a few months ago at a bar, so he gave her the impression that he owned the Galaxy and was pretty well off. He probably should have picked someone else to share his non-existent good fortune with, although she is very pretty.

I knew Steve was good in a fight, but I was still amazed when he moved with lightning speed and pushed his date's pistol into the air while also kicking the one out of my date's hand. It didn't stop his date from fighting back though. She kneed him in the stomach—twice. He finally pulled the gun out of her hand, but not before it accidentally fired into the ceiling several times. The crowd panicked and stampeded out of the club once they figured out what was happening. I didn't think so many people could leave the building that quickly, but I was wrong. I guess my date wasn't as interested in fighting as her friend, because she disappeared into the crowd.

Steve pointed the gun at his date to stop her from fighting. She just smiled and followed after her friend without saying a word. We were going to follow after them, but the local police force arrived before we could leave.

The police questioned us for a few hours at their station until the captain arrived to pick us up. He wasn't happy about having to leave his weightlifting competition, but I don't think he needed another trophy to add to his collection anyway. He already has eight of them. How many does he really need?

Anyway, the next time Steve asks me to go on a double date with him, I think I'll say no. Well, unless he throws in dinner too. Who can resist a free meal?

Goober, out.

HOT GIRL
FEATURING STEVE

Ship's log.

I'm not usually one to kiss and tell, but the captain insisted I give my account of what happened on Bentazi Urama for the log. Since Goober pretty much filled in my part, I thought I'd go over how I met my date a few months ago. I've gotta warn you though, my moves aren't for amateurs. Use what I tell you for informational purposes only. I can't be held responsible if you end up in jail or the medical center for trying out my techniques. You've been warned.

So, I was at this club back on Karamii Station about three months ago waiting for the ship to be repaired when I met her. She had long, flowing purple hair with deep green highlights. I remember doing a double take at her form-fitting, dark purple dress as she danced in the middle of the room. I wasn't exactly sure if it was even a dress at first or just awesome body paint, but I sure as heck had every intention of finding out.

I left my Firestorm beer at the counter and started moving toward her but then stopped, returned to the bar, and pounded back the rest of my drink. Those damn things cost 30 credits at that place, and there was absolutely no way I was going to let my money get flushed down the drain.

After that was settled, I adjusted my lucky silver belt and approached her. She was dancing with some jerk that had moves like an insect on fire, so I tapped the loser on the shoulder and cut in front of him when he turned around. I was doing the girl a favor by getting rid of that mud stain, but he apparently didn't think so. I barely had time to give her my usual "hey, babe" intro when Mr. Floppy tapped me on the shoulder.

"Hey, that's my date!" the idiot protested.

I just told him to buzz off and began showing everyone in the club how a real man danced. The girl was just starting to dig my moves when I felt a tug on my left arm. I turned around to face the buzz kill when he took a swing at me. This guy was at least six inches shorter than I was and wore a pair of Jura-Pa goggles. Don't get me wrong, the goggles are cool, but not on this shmuck and definitely not on a date. They probably would have looked better on the barstool than on his ugly mug.

Normally, I would have pounded this guy into the ground for attacking me. Since I wanted to show my new date how cool I was, I grabbed the guy's fist and threw it back in his face. He hit himself squarely on the nose and it started gushing like a broken sewage pipe. He grabbed his leaking honker and said something to the effect of "you'll pay for this," but it was hard to tell exactly what he said with his muffled voice. Finally, the guy ran off into the crowd and disappeared, leaving me to spend some quality time with my new date.

I apologized to the girl for having to suffer through that goggled bozo. She just shook her head and laughed, telling me I probably shouldn't have done that. Her eyes were a mesmerizing light blue, like a beautiful cloudless sky. I wasn't really paying attention to what she said at first though since I was too busy checking her out, so I had to ask her to repeat herself. When she did, I told her not to worry about it. She shrugged and pressed her body against mine as we moved to the beat of the pulsing music. She was a great dancer, and wasn't shy about getting up close and personal with someone she just met. It…was…awesome!

Like all awesome things though, this one had to come to an end, sooner or later. I only wish it was later. We had only been dancing for ten minutes or so when she motioned behind me and told me I should probably go. I would have been insane to leave this terrific woman after only ten minutes with her, but as it turned out, she was right.

When I turned around, her former date was headed straight toward me, only this time he was sandwiched between five hulking guys with muscles the size of massive boulders. None of them looked very happy, and I had the feeling that they were about to try to make me feel the same way.

The girl told me that her former date was Jural Jura-Pa. That's right, he was the inventor of the goggles and other popular combat gear that were preferred among freelancers, soldiers, and guys just wanting to impress their friends. How was I supposed to know the guy had more money than the government treasury? He just looked like some nutball trying to impress a girl that was way too hot for him to handle. I guess the saying "you can't judge a weapon by its size" really is true after all. Who knew?

Before they reached me, I stole a kiss from the beautiful woman. Her lips were as soft and inviting as they looked, but the amazing experience didn't last long. Two of the thugs pulled me away from her before I could even get her name. They dragged me toward the exit with the other three muscle heads in tow, just in case I resisted. I may be good with my fists and always ready for a good fight, but I'm not crazy. Resistance wasn't an option.

Just as the behemoths were about to toss me out of the club, I spotted Jural dancing with the lovely goddess again. He placed his thumbs in his ears and wiggled his fingers while poking his tongue in my direction. Classy guy. I started to turn away to see where I was about to be thrown when the woman winked at me. I barely had time to blow her a kiss in response before I the goons tossed out the front door.

As I landed hard on the ground outside, I thought about the stunning woman I had just met. I don't think I've ever met anyone quite like her, and I've met quite a few women in my time. I picked myself up, dusted off my awesome brown jacket, and tried to call the ship to check on its status. That's when I found out that my wristcom was missing. I looked at the ground I had been intimate with a few moments ago to search for it when I remembered the girl inside. Her hands had been all over me, and it was possible, just possible that she had taken it. I checked my jacket pocket and found that my credit purse was missing too.

She was good, I'll give her that. I'd like to say that I was angry about it, but really, I probably would have still danced with her even if I'd known she was a thief. Her profession just made her even hotter, especially since it explains why she stayed with that goggled dork when she could have had a stud like me. I still wonder how much she managed to siphon away from him. Whatever it was, he deserved it for the rude gesture he gave me at the end of the night.

By the way, in case you're wondering, her dress *was* painted on. It's supposed to be a new fashion that's all the rage with women this year. The thick paint is sprayed over a bikini base, leaving little to the imagination. I love it, and I hope to see even more of it—or less of it, if you catch my drift. Ha!

Steve, out.

HACK OFF
FEATURING JONN BROCK

Ship's log.

I'm not a big fan of recording what happens during my off hours, but Captain Mintax insisted I give my account of what happened on the planet. I can only hope nobody listens to this until long after I'm gone. Never would be better, but I'm not usually that lucky.

The crew and I had just landed on the planet Bentazi Urama when I received a call from the High Aptitude Coalition for Knowledge and Enhanced Research Systems. I wondered how they knew about my arrival so soon, but then I remembered it was one of the most notorious computer infiltration and retrieval organizations in this sector of the galaxy. They usually know about a ship's arrival before its captain even knows the destination.

I was hesitant to take the call at first since I refused their invitation to join the Coalition a few years ago. I can't recall the last time someone refused to join them, and I was lucky they didn't take offense at my decision. Since they never came after me, I just assumed they forgot I existed. Their call to me on the planet proved otherwise.

There really wasn't any point in hiding from them, so I took the call. If it came down to it, my crewmates would do whatever they could to help me out of a jam. I'm not sure it would have done much good against this particular group, but it was at least some form of reassurance, and a whole heck of a lot better than nothing.

To my surprise, the group didn't bear any malice toward me. In fact, it was quite the opposite. They had been tracking my exploits aboard the Galaxy, and were impressed with my accomplishments. That was a huge relief to hear, and I thanked them for the compliment. I was hoping that was the only reason for the call, but it wasn't it.

They invited me to join the intergalactic Cyber Intrusion Contest they were holding that very night. It was part of the larger festivities on the planet celebrating the accomplishments of every thief, pirate, and scam artist in this part of the galaxy. My friends join in on the annual weekend celebration each year, but this is the first time I've had the opportunity to go with them.

I wasn't sure about participating in the contest at first, but then I thought about what might happen if I refused the invitation. After briefly considering my options, I graciously accepted the request.

The contest arena consisted of three ten-point stars arranged in a triangular pattern. At each point, an elaborate crescent-shaped computer platform faced toward the center of its star. There were no chairs and the arrangement of the workstations ensured that each contestant could clearly see the others. That also meant that everyone could see each other's holographic display screen and copy their work if they wanted to. Talk about pressure.

When the contest began, each group received a different live computer challenge. My group was tasked with infiltrating the combat control system aboard the Tioran Federation drone carrier Oberious. I'm familiar with Federation programming code and cyber defenses, but I've never gained access to one of their carrier combat systems before. I was looking forward to the challenge, but judging by the expressions on the faces of the other contestants, I'd say they were more interested in crushing each other than anything else.

I used my standard approach to penetrating the Oberious' systems one by one. It's just like peeling an onion. I'm willing to bet that the others used a more straightforward approach. From my experience though, exploiting weaknesses in lesser-defended systems could make accessing the heavily defended systems easier. I noticed several of the other contestants watching me do my work, but I wasn't concerned. I could see what they were working on, and there was nothing I was doing that could have helped them out of their messes.

Many people in my profession either don't know about the intensity of military electronic countermeasures or they arrogantly think that they can easily beat them. One of these defense systems is designed to detect an intrusion, trace the signal, and send a pulse wave feedback charge toward the point of origin. It not only destroys the hackers' computer; it might even incinerate the person trying to break into the system.

One by one, the other contestants were shocked away from their terminals. The contest sponsors must have installed a pulse wave nullifier in each station, or I doubt anyone would have survived the feedback. It finally came down to just me and one other contestant directly across from me. I could see from the reverse angle of his terminal that he was using a similar approach to mine in accessing the Oberious. He was good, and I was having trouble with the ancillary current router attached to the combat system. I knew that if I couldn't find a way to reroute power to the intrusion system, he would probably win. That's when I came up with the perfect solution.

I quickly made adjustments to the router and activated the defense system. Normally, this wouldn't have been a good thing since I would have been shocked away from my terminal. Fortunately, I managed to use the defense system to my advantage by redirecting the pulse wave to my competitor. He was instantly shocked away from his terminal while simultaneously giving me access to the combat system. I won the contest in my star arena in record time.

The winners of each star normally face off

against each other to figure out who the grand champion is going to be, but all of the other 20 contestants failed to complete their objective. The contest sponsors had thrown in a twist to this year's match, pitting the contestants in the other two star groups against mine. It didn't exactly sound fair to me, so that's probably why they failed to mention it before the match.

I ended up winning a computer terminal just like the one used in the contest as a prize, plus a lifetime honorary membership in the HACKERS group. I couldn't exactly refuse membership a second time, so I accepted. I just hope they never call me for assistance in one of their highly illegal projects. I doubt the captain would appreciate my involvement *unless* it came with a big payday.

Jonn, out.

SLIMEBALL MERCHANT
FEATURING GLENDA RITAN

Ship's log.

It's been a while since I've had a little time to myself. There's always one problem or another to deal with on this ship—or with my friends. Our recent trip to Bentazi Urama was supposed to be an opportunity to relax for a change. Unfortunately, it turned out to be anything but the vacation I hoped it would be.

After we landed on the planet and the guys went off to do whatever it was they did, I used their absence to do a little shopping in the bazaar. If you've never been to the bazaar, I highly recommend it. They have everything you can think of there and a few items you've never even heard about before. Be sure to take along strong negotiating skills and a nose for detecting manure though, or you'll likely walk away with useless junk and empty pockets.

I've been to many of these places before, so I knew my way around. I had a list of parts we needed for the ship, and I enjoyed the process of selecting the best items available for the least amount possible. Some people might think shopping for engineering equipment on vacation defeats the purpose of the visit, but I think they're wrong. Haggling for gear is actually therapeutic for me. It's a relaxing change of pace with a process I can control, unlike some of the messes we usually find ourselves in aboard the ship. Try it for yourself some time if you doubt me. You might be surprised at how much you enjoy it.

We don't usually have much of a budget for the items we need on the ship, and slightly used parts are more of a luxury than an affordable alternative. I typically pick among the leftovers to compensate—items that nobody in their right mind would rely on for their spacecraft. I can usually tweak them to suit our purposes for a while, but one of these days, I'd like to know what it feels like to shop with more than hopes and dreams in my pocket. Dare to dream, I guess.

When I arrived at one particular outdoor

shop, the collection of power regulators in stock didn't quite meet my needs. I was about to move on when the merchant asked me what I wanted. I gave him the specifications of the module I needed, and to my surprise, he said he had just received a delivery recently that might contain what I was after. He didn't have the chance to sort through the items yet, so he invited me inside his shop to search through them.

Shoppers throughout the massive bazaar were constantly in and out of other shops, so I didn't think anything of the suggestion, at least not at first. When I walked inside, the room was fairly spacious. It was filled with a massive collection of used parts lining tall, dusty shelves with some of the more choice items resting inside illuminated display cases. The narrow paths through the merchandise made maneuvering through them almost claustrophobic, but I was used to cramped spaces inside some of the narrow system access passages aboard the Galaxy.

When we arrived at the counter near the rear of the shop, he held open a gray curtain and invited me into the back room. I hesitated, considering the darkness of the room beyond as a perfect place for an ambush. I'm no stranger to dangerous situations, and I can more than handle myself in a fight. Still, if experience has taught me anything, it's to avoid the unknown in the absence of competent backup. Since my friends were far away, backup wasn't an option.

I asked the merchant if he could get the part I needed and bring it outside. That's when his smile faded. He called out into the shop, and with whisper silent movements, two hulking men appeared behind me. They had probably been lurking in the shadowy depths of the shop, waiting for a target for whatever it was they were planning. I had no interest in being a part of their plans.

I thanked the shopkeeper for his help and told him that I didn't need the part after all. I turned to leave, but the men blocked my path. They smelled heavily of dirt and oil, so I guess it must have been a while since they last stepped outside—or showered. When they smiled, their yellowed, crusty teeth were a painful sight to see, and their breaths weren't any better. I asked them politely to step out of my way, but I guess my request meant something else in their language because they reached out for me and tried to force me into the next room.

I immediately went for my sidearm, but the

shopkeeper beat me to it. He pointed my own weapon at me and gestured to the room behind him with it. I knew that if I entered the room, there was no way I was leaving, at least not alive.

I sized up the two gentlemen blocking my path and tried to determine my chances of fighting my way past them. Given their massive and somewhat sloppy bulk, I wasn't sure I could take them down before the merchant could shoot me with my gun. I needed an edge, and I saw just the right one.

I grabbed a solid, half-meter length of water flow piping from the wall that was mixed in with other items on display and slammed it into the jaws of both oily thugs in one swing. The men crashed to the ground, stunned from the blow. I don't think that slimeball of a merchant expected the move because he appeared just as stunned as his men. I used his inaction to thrust the end of the pipe into his stomach and knocked him backward into the dark room. I picked up my gun that he had dropped onto the floor, set it to immobilize, and fired at the two hulking slugs while they struggled to stand up.

On my way out of the shop, I saw the part I needed inside one of the glass display cases. Using the handle of my pistol, I smashed open the case, grabbed the part, and returned to the street to finish my shopping. I don't normally take items that belong to someone else, but I figured I more than paid for the part when the merchant detained me against my will. It's the least he owed me for my time, and I dare anyone to tell me otherwise.

Like I said earlier, it wasn't exactly a relaxing vacation, but it sure was an interesting one.

Hitch, out.

STACK MASTER
FEATURING CAPTAIN MINTAX

Ship's log.

I almost never say this, and I'm not likely to repeat it again, but when I had to bail Steve and Goober out of jail recently, I was glad for the disruption.

It started when we landed on Bentazi Urama, the black market capital in this arm of the galaxy. One of the main reasons I even bother showing up at this toilet bowl of a planet is the yearly weightlifting competition. The Urama Ultima invites the strongest athletes from every shadowy corner of the galaxy and throws them in the same arena to test their prowess against each other. Most of these slimeballs come for the 100,000 credit prize awarded to the champion with the most points. I do it for the pleasure of beating these bums back to whatever holes they crawled out of. Well, that and the prize money. I have to pay for docking fees somehow.

When I arrived in the locker room at the arena, I recognized a few of the oil stains from previous matches. They thought they could top me then, and they were wrong. I came away with the trophy eight years in a row. There was no way I was going to let them beat me this year either.

The snarls and deathly stares I received from them were all the encouragement I needed. In my experience, the guys who hate me that much are usually jealous of what I have. It makes them feel better to do what they can to intimidate me, boosting their self-confidence. These jerkoffs never have what it takes to beat me, and as long as I can keep getting that kind of response out of them, I know the trophy is as good as mine.

There were a few unfamiliar faces in the room this year. None seemed like much of a challenge, but there was one that I met once before outside the competition. I ran into him at a fitness center on Darius Station in the Ugama cluster. I hate to admit it, but he was impressive. Every time I jacked up the weight on my bench bar, so did he—only he added more than I did. At the end of the workout, he came over to shake my hand and told me I had great form. I told him thanks, but that was it. I don't recall the last time someone out-lifted me, and I wasn't about to give him the satisfaction of kicking my rear in the impromptu competition.

Now, here he was again, but this time the competition was real, and he was after my trophy. I wasn't about to let him have it without a fight. I will give him this though; he's one heck of a sportsman. Just before we moved into the arena, he came over and shook my hand. That's when he did the worst thing anybody could have done before the match. He wished me luck. Can you believe that? Of all the dirty things he could have pulled. What the heck was he thinking? I decided right then and there that he was dead meat, so of course, I repeated the underhanded move. Two can play at that game.

By the time we reached the halfway mark in the competition though, it was clear that he had the upper hand. I had 42 points to his 48. The next competitor's highest score was 31, and just as I thought, nobody else proved to be much of a challenge. Unless I managed to step up my game and quick, it wouldn't matter how far I was ahead of the rest of the competition. This guy was going to win, leaving me in second place. I *never* settle for second place.

Fortunately, the next event was one where I always crush the competition. It was the cargo stack challenge and took a few brain cells, as well as brawn, to finish. The object of the challenge is to stack cargo containers of different weights on colored platforms adjacent to a series of multi-directional stairs. Contestants are supposed to figure out the weight of each container and place all ten of them on a platform that can handle that weight. Just before the match, the competition director tells each participant the amount of weight a color can handle for his or her round, and all platform weights and colors are randomized after each round to prevent cheating by the next lifter. During the match, if a lifter places a container on a platform that can't hold its weight, the platform collapses, and the round is over. Judges award one point for each container successfully placed on a platform and a bonus point for each successful placement if a lifter places all containers correctly.

This event was my chance to pull ahead.

As I expected, most of the blowhards in

the group failed to stack more than three of the containers. Those are the guys who mouthed off the most before the match. They just never seem to learn that it takes more than juiced muscles to win this competition. Personally, I don't touch that crap they infuse into their bodies. I want my wins to be all mine, and I won't let artificial enhancements dictate my success.

None of the remaining guys stacked more than eight of the containers before screwing up on the last two. When it was my turn, I showed those juiceheads just how a real pro should do it. I even beat my personal best time too. My humiliating defeat of the others didn't last though. That bastard I met at the station was up next, and he blasted through the course in record time. It's a good thing they don't award bonus points for the fastest time or I would have had no chance to win. Still, I was down six points, and there were only two events left. If I didn't think of something fast, I was going to lose my first contest in eight years.

Sometimes luck comes in mysterious ways. For me, that way is usually none at all. This time, however, it came in the form of Goober and Steve. Just before the start of the last match, one of the judges came up and told me local authorities requested my presence at their station. I made up one point over Mr. Perfect in the previous match, but I was still down by five. Unless he completely screwed up in the last event, he was going to win. Under normal circumstances, I would have told the judge that Goober and Steve could just sit there and wait until I finished the competition. Given that I was about to lose my first contest in nearly a decade, I felt compelled to withdraw from the Ultima and report to the station.

I've never backed down from a challenge before, but I wasn't about to ignore a way out of this one. To add insult to injury, Mr. Perfect came over just before I left the arena and apologized that we couldn't finish the match together. He extended his hand in a show of support. Where the heck did he think he was? We were on a planet packed with thieves and cutthroats. There's no place for sportsmanship here. Still, I shook his hand anyway. I think his grip was even stronger than mine. No matter. For me, the match was over, and I avoided my first loss. There's no sense in being a gracious loser if you can avoid it, and I did.

Mintax, out.

The End

EXCERPT FROM
GALAXY CHRONICLES VOL. 1
DRONE WARS II

Captain Mintax raised his rifle, sighted his target, and pressed the trigger button. A blue plasma burst launched from the assault weapon and bolted down the long, green hallway.

A black, egg-shaped drone hovered in the air at the opposite end of the corridor tracking the movements of the Starcruiser Galaxy's crew when it detected the impending threat. It darted out of the path of the approaching blast, deftly removing itself from the calculated trajectory. The plasma burst noted the altered location of its target and adjusted its course to compensate. The drone did its best to move itself out of harm's way once more, but it was too late. The plasma burst slammed into the drone, obliterating the tiny craft.

"See? I told you these new rifles were awesome," Steve commented, stroking the black and chrome barrel of the gun as if it was his favorite pet.

Mintax shot a skeptical glance at his weapons expert before he returned his attention to the shattered remains of the drone. "You never did tell me how much they cost."

Steve knew the captain wouldn't approve of the purchase price, so he quickly changed the subject. "We should probably concentrate on getting rid of these drones before they take over the ship." He looked over his shoulder at Jonn. "How many of these things did you say there were?"

Mintax growled and assumed that his weapons specialist grossly overpaid for the four new rifles. If there was one thing the thrifty captain hated more than anything, it was paying more than his perceived value for something, regardless of actual worth.

Jonn cut into the man's thoughts. "I only created one prototype, but it reprogrammed the assembler to create more."

"So you don't know how many there are?" Mintax asked in annoyance.

Jonn shook his head. "Sorry, Captain."

"That's okay," Goober interjected. "They're not armed like the ones in the game. It shouldn't be too hard to get rid of them."

Jonn rubbed the back of his neck and looked at the Galaxy's communications specialist with a pained expression. "Well, they're probably not going to stay that way."

"What's that supposed to mean?" Mintax asked, uncertain whether he wanted to know the answer.

Jonn inhaled deeply before explaining. "I patterned the drone after the game Drone Wars. You know, the one I've been spending a lot of my free time playing?"

Mintax glared.

"Um, anyway," Jonn continued, "I thought we could use a drone on this ship to help with maintenance and, you know, to keep me company."

"You made yourself a pet?" Steve said.

Jonn nodded. "Sort of, yeah. I extracted the base code from the game's program and used that as a starting point to create a simple artificial intelligence for the drone. I wanted it to look and feel like the drones in the game but without the killer instinct."

Three drones appeared at the end of the corridor and scanned the remains of their companion. The single, glowing eye at the tip of their bodies turned a darker shade of green as they focused their attention on the Galaxy's crew. Each of the drone's dual tentacles pointed at their new enemy and fired a barrage of yellow laser bursts.

The crew ducked behind the safety of the T-junction walls to avoid the incoming fire.

"I thought you said you programmed them without a killer instinct?" Steve contended.

Jonn swallowed nervously. "I did, and I didn't. Their base program came with three settings: unarmed and unshielded, armed and unshielded, and armed and shielded. They were meant to give a player progressively more difficult levels to choose from in the game. I kept them in the drone's program, just in case we needed it to help us repel intruders, but I set the prototype at level 1. I don't know what happened."

"Your pet grew teeth," Mintax said. "What other surprises should I expect?"

"If they follow the progression of the game, then they probably just upgraded to level two. That means we can still take them out."

"What happens if they get to level three?" Goober asked.

"That would be bad," Jonn said. "Our

weapons probably wouldn't penetrate their shields, at least not right away."

Steve steadied his rifle. "Then let's take these bastards out before that happens." He looked at the captain and nodded.

Mintax and Steve moved into the hall, sighted their targets, and fired a series of bursts from their plasma rifles. The drones spotted their prey and returned fire. One of the laser blasts struck Mintax's left arm before he and Steve could return to the safety of the junction. A fraction of a second later, they heard several explosions as the plasma bursts annihilated their targets.

Goober peeked around the corner and inspected the damage. "You got 'em, Captain." He looked at Mintax and saw a small hole with singed edges in his brown shirt. "Captain, you're shot."

"I'm fine," Mintax said through gritted teeth. He narrowed his eyes at Jonn. "Where's your assembler?"

"Engineering."

"That's three decks down," Steve said in disbelief. "Holy crap, they're trying to take over the damn ship if they made it all the way up here."

Mintax moved into the corridor to trace the direction of the drones. "Then we're going down there to take them out before that happens."

"We should probably fix your arm first," Goober commented, bringing attention back to the captain's arm.

Mintax shook his head. "Later. I want that assembler destroyed and those drone bastards off my ship first."

"Once we get to engineering, I can shut down the assembler and purge the drone's design specs." Jonn assured. "If we're lucky, we can—."

"No!" Mintax interrupted. "The code is still in that damn thing, and I want it destroyed. Is that clear?"

Jonn's shoulders slumped. He spent six weeks creating the nano-assembler to help him design and construct his prototype creations. He wasn't at all happy to learn of its imminent destruction. "But Captain, if I purge the program from the device, we can still use it to create other new technologies."

"If that technology is anything like these drones of yours, no thanks," Steve said.

Mintax shook his head. "I'm not taking any chances. When we get to engineering, we're taking it out."

"Yes, Captain," Jonn responded in disappointment.

The crew slowly walked to the intra-ship transport chamber at the end of the corridor and moved inside.

"Hmm, that's odd." Goober scratched the side of his head in confusion.

"What is?" Steve asked.

Mintax moved to enter the sequence for transport to engineering.

"Well, if they're as smart as they are in the game, you'd think the drones would try to stop us from getting to engineering. That is their base of operations, so to speak. Isn't it?"

Mintax paused before tapping the final button on the chamber control pad. "He's right. Those bastards probably have a trap waiting for us when we get there."

"Good," Steve replied. "With all of those things clustered in one area, it'll be hard for even Goober to miss."

Goober folded his arms indignantly and grunted. "Humph."

"Yeah, and it'll be hard for them to miss us too," Mintax added.

Steve sighed. "Fine. Then if we can't blast our way through them, I've got another idea that might just do the trick."

To read more of this exciting adventure, go to http://www.starcruisergalaxy.com.

ABOUT THE AUTHOR

Rod has a passion for testing the limits of the improbable. His desire to explore the unknown is born from a love of science fiction that began when he was but a mere seedling on another plane of existence. Whether that consists of transcendence or daydreaming behind a desk is still a matter of heated debate.

Beyond a strong appetite for writing fiction, Rod also manages the fraud defense website ownyourdefense.net, blogs for several websites, and enjoys testing the tensile strength of gym equipment. When the construction of fantastic universes with his mechanical keyboard won't satiate his burning desire to create, a heavy set of dumbbells or learning a new fraud prevention technique will do.

To learn more about Rod's other cosmic journeys, be sure to check out www.starcruisergalaxy.com. While visiting the website, you'll find more information about the crew, puzzles, summaries of the Adventures of the Starcruiser Galaxy novels, as well as audio and video logs. You'll also find links to other exciting adventures with the Starcruiser Galaxy and its crew including the novellas *A Very Goober Christmas, The Wereghost Menace, The Vampire Clones of Clegz, and Brakka's Zombie Armada,* a collection of 12 short stories in *Galaxy Chronicles Vol. 1,* as well as the novel *Who Blew Up My Ship.*

Dream big, and the universe will be your playground.

CONNECT WITH ROD:

Twitter: http://twitter.com/RodSpurgeon
Pinterest: http://pinterest.com/rodspurgeon
Facebook: http://facebook.com/Rod.Spurgeon
Website: http://www.starcruisergalaxy.com

GALAXY DIARIES
WORD SEARCH

Y	J	H	P	U	T	K	M	Q	G	M	I	D	O	E
T	W	M	A	A	K	O	Y	U	E	I	I	E	G	D
M	K	E	G	G	C	I	R	V	O	N	M	T	R	B
L	I	A	L	T	G	A	Z	U	M	E	A	A	A	F
Z	N	N	S	A	T	L	T	A	I	R	R	L	C	D
Y	U	I	I	A	D	S	I	L	T	S	A	O	Z	U
N	R	A	N	N	W	R	R	N	E	N	K	S	F	R
W	Q	I	N	W	G	Q	I	E	G	D	E	I	B	A
F	U	N	A	I	S	I	L	A	T	H	G	B	A	T
M	S	P	O	R	T	S	M	A	N	S	H	I	P	A
L	L	A	B	E	C	R	O	F	C	S	A	P	U	N
O	B	E	R	I	O	U	S	L	G	X	D	L	O	I
E	T	S	A	W	H	A	C	K	E	R	S	F	B	U
V	P	I	P	E	X	V	T	P	J	X	A	W	I	M
M	J	V	R	B	X	Q	A	E	D	N	S	J	J	J

Alisian
Apex
Bentazi
Blasters
Cargo
Delta
Duratanium
Forceball
Geomite
Guratanium
Hackers
Haggling

Isolated
Karamii
Miners
Mining
Oberious
Pipe
Sportsmanship
Tagan
Uki
Waste
Weladrians
Wristcom

Scan this QR
code for a
helpful hint in
solving the
word search.